Library of Congress Cataloging in Publication Data:
Cosgrove, Stephen. Gobble and gulp. (A Whimsie storybook) SUMMARY: Twin Whimsies Blossom and Sprout, under a spell from the Switch Witch, ignore the foods that are good for them and stuff themselves with sweet desserts. 1. Children's stories, American. [1. Food habits—Fiction. 2. Twins—Fiction. 3. Witches–Fiction.] I. Reasoner, Charles, ill. II. Title. III. Series: Cosgrove, Stephen. Whimsie storybook. PZ7.C8187Go 1985 [E] 85-42715 ISBN: 0-394-87457-9

Manufactured in Belgium
1 2 3 4 5 6 7 8 9 0

The Whimsies™
STORYBOOKS

Gobble and Gulp

by Stephen Cosgrove

illustrated by Charles Reasoner

Random House 🏠 New York

Have you ever watched a bird fly so high in the sky that it becomes just a tiny dot and then disappears? Have you ever wondered where it goes or maybe wondered why? If you could wing along with that bird you would come to the Land of Whim.

In this magical place you would find the jagged peaks of the Quirk Mountains. Far below, beside the River Whim, was a lush, green valley. And in this valley lived furry little

creatures called Whimsies. The Whimsies had cute button noses and bright, shiny eyes, and were covered from head to foot with fur as soft as dandelion down.

They worked here. They played here. They slept and they dreamed here. For this was and always would be the home of the Whimsies beside the River Whim, beneath the Quirk Mountains.

All the Whimsies—and there were many—loved to work in their gardens. Day after day in spring, summer, and fall they would plant and weed and hoe. And oh, the plants they would grow: raspberries, blueberries, tomatoes, potatoes, long string beans, carrots, and peas. The Whimsies grew all sorts of fruits and vegetables, and here and there a flower or two.

There was one thing the Whimsies loved even more than working in their gardens. And that was eating all the good, wholesome foods that they grew. They would eat lovely green salads of clover and kale, fresh-cooked corn, and hot vegetable soup. At any time of day you could find at least one Whimsie munching on a carrot or eating a juicy apple.

As an extra-special treat, they might have a piece of honey-apple cake or rhubarb pie, but only once in a while, because they knew that too many sweets were not good for them.

Blossom and Sprout were little Whimsie twins, and like all good Whimsies, they loved to eat their vegetables. That is, any vegetable except turnips! The twins hated turnips.

While the rest of the family was eating a lip-smacking dinner of fried turnip pie, Blossom and Sprout would feed their turnips to Woolly Woofer, the Whimsies' only dog. Woolly didn't like turnips either, and when the dinner was done you could always find a whole mess of turnips under the table.

One night at dinner Blossom and Sprout refused to take one single bite of steaming turnip stew. Their parents were so annoyed that they made the twins clean up the kitchen—every pot and pan—even though it wasn't their turn.

The twins grumbled and mumbled as they scrubbed and scoured. They were so caught up in their grumbling that they were nearly scared out of their wits by the sudden appearance of a strange old lady with a lizard at her side.

"Who are you?" they asked in unison.

"Well . . ." said the old crone, "you might think of me as the Sugarplum Fairy, but my friends—and I have many—call me Switch Witch. And this is my pet, Wizard Lizard. I've come searching for the twins who hate turnips!"

"That's us!" they chimed together. "We can't stand turnips!"

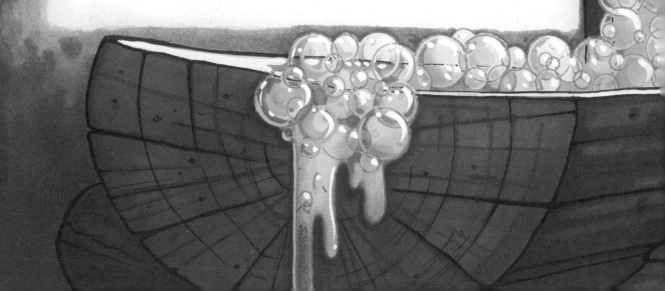

"Well, well, well!" said Switch Witch wickedly. "This must be your lucky day, because I have a magical charm for each of you. As long as the charm is worn around your neck you will never have to eat turnips again!"

With that she reached into a deep pocket in her skirt and pulled out two necklaces. Both of the necklaces had a white, sugarcoated tooth dangling from a chain of licorice. "They are called Sweet Tooth necklaces. When you wear them, something wonderful happens. You will be able to eat lots and lots of sugary, sweet foods."

"But the old Whimsies always say that too many sweets are bad for us!" protested the twins.

Switch Witch waved the charms from side to side and said, "How can anything this sweet be bad?"

Blossom and Sprout thought about that, but they couldn't come up with an answer. So they quickly put on the Sweet Tooth necklaces. Then—poof!—just like that, Switch Witch and Wizard Lizard disappeared in a swirl of cotton candy.

All of a sudden Blossom and Sprout felt hungry, very, very hungry. They looked all over the kitchen for something to eat. They saw some carrots and apples, but that wasn't what they wanted. Then they found a box of sugar clover cookies. What fun! They did not stop eating until every single cookie was gone. Gobble and gulp! Blossom and Sprout even ate up all the crumbs.

The next day Blossom and Sprout had no appetite for breakfast, lunch, or dinner. They picked at a bit of this and a bit of that, but they ate very little—very little, that is, until they came to a dessert of dandelion pie or carrot cake surprise. Then they ate, and oh, how they ate. Gobble and gulp!

Mama and Papa Whimsie finally refused to give the twins any dessert until they ate all their supper. But that didn't stop Blossom and Sprout, and right after the meal they rushed to their bedroom where they had hidden all sorts of

treats! There were cookies and cakes, pastries and pies, and even a layer cake three stories high. All of it was eaten in the flash of an eye. Gobble and gulp!

Blossom and Sprout kept eating sweet after sweet. They even gobbled and gulped spaghetti topped with chocolate sauce, followed by a cookie crumb salad with whipped cream dressing. Gobble and gulp!

Mama and Papa were exhausted from trying to get Blossom and Sprout to eat some good food. One day they invited Grandma Whimsie, one of the oldest and wisest Whimsies, over to the house to talk about what to do.

"We have got to stop them," Mama Whimsie said.

"They'll get sick if they eat any more sweets!" said Papa.

Finally Grandma Whimsie spoke. "By any chance, are the twins wearing new necklaces?" she asked.

"Why, yes!" said Mama and Papa.

"They are under the magic spell of Switch Witch's Sweet Tooth charms," said Grandma Whimsie. "The only way to stop the magic is to get the twins to brush the Sweet Tooth and see what lies beneath the white sugar coating."

With that she set out to find the twins and break the spell.

Grandma Whimsie found the twins sitting in their room still gobbling and gulping. "You must stop eating all these sweets!" Grandma Whimsie said. "They're not good for you."

"Never!" said the twins together, as they gobbled and gulped. "Besides, how can anything this sweet be bad for you?"

"Ahh," said old Grandma Whimsie gently but firmly, "why don't you brush your Sweet Tooth and see what lies within?"

Blossom went into the bathroom, took her toothbrush, and with Sprout watching, began to brush the Sweet Tooth. As the magical white sugar fell away they could see that the Sweet Tooth was not so white underneath. It was dark and decayed.

To their dismay, they realized that all the sweet foods they had been eating were not good for them at all. With their tummies aching from eating all those sweets, they took off the Sweet Tooth necklaces and threw them far away.

One day, a short time later, Wizard Lizard, who had been sent to the woods to look for brightly colored stones, happened upon the Sweet Tooth charms. Silly creature that he was, he put them both on. With a craving for sugar and sweets, he rushed back to Switch Witch castle and tried to eat her out of house and home.

All returned to normal in the Land of Whim as the Whimsie twins, Blossom and Sprout, went back to eating good and wholesome food. Although they still couldn't stand turnips, at least they tried to eat them once in a while.

Blossom and Sprout
Know that sweets
taste yummy,
But too many
of them
Are bad for
your tummy.